Preface

Daniel and Chloe had experienced some amazing adventures after finding an old compass on the beach. They soon discovered that this compass was no ordinary compass, and could take them back to any time period they wanted.

While in search for the creator of the compass, the mysterious Professor Bailey; the brother and sister duo went back to Roman time Chester, were accidentally involved in a siege at a castle, met an old pirate ancestor and had some encounters with a notorious highwayman. They also discovered that the compass allowed them to go back in time as invisible spirits, where they could also see real-life ghosts, and they could make themselves appear and disappear. After they had seen real-life ghosts, they found that they could then see them whether they were in "invisible mode" or not. An old cavalier ghost called Charles had helped them on a couple of occasions.

They finally found Professor Bailey, after breaking the compass and getting stuck in the past. He rescued them from a murderous highwayman and then gave them two brand new compasses that could also move in space as well as time; they could go anywhere in the world in any time period they wanted to go. The compasses were linked together so that the children could contact the Professor, should they ever need to.

Contents

Chapter 1: Forest adventure

Daniel and Chloe sat looking at the shiny new compasses, given to them by the Professor, and thought about where and when in time to go. Daniel had dreams about learning to train as a knight, and Chloe wanted to travel the world to see famous civilisations.

The Professor had told them how us their compasses to get to certain places, so as a test, they aimed to go to a nearby forest just a few miles away. Daniel and Chloe stood side by side each with their compasses.

"Here goes nothing!" said Daniel.

He moved the slider and they were both transported to the forest. They knew they must be still in their own time as a modern diesel engine thundered past, along the forest railway line.

"OK" said Daniel. "That worked OK, now to see if we can move back in time and stay in the same place".

Chloe turned the button on her compass and saw that the railway line had now gone and forest seemed denser with more undergrowth, they were back in time.

Daniel and Chloe suddenly heard a strange snuffling sound; it was right behind where they were standing. They turned thinking it must be a dog; but were shocked to face a pig-like animal with huge tusks.

"What on earth is it?" gasped Chloe.

"I think it's a wild boar" said Daniel, "There used to be lots in the forest at one time, the kings of the past would come to hunt them".

Daniel used the compass to appear to the boar. The boar jumped in shock and then ran off into the dense undergrowth of the forest.

"Daniel!" scolded Chloe, "I think we should stay invisible, who knows what dangers might be here..." However, before she could finish she saw some glowing yellow eyes in the darkness of the trees behind Daniel.

Within a second, the creature leaped out into the light and was revealed as a huge wolf. It growled and had drool foaming at the edges of its mouth. The children didn't have time to get their compasses out to escape, and started to run for their lives.

They ran quickly, but the wolf was close behind them and was nearly on top of them. Then something odd happened. The growling wolf suddenly gave out a yelp, and the sound of pursuing paws came to a sudden halt.

Daniel and Chloe turned to see that an arrow had been fired at the wolf. It was alive, but was pulling at the arrow in its side with its teeth.

"Quick children, that's only slowed him down!" urged a man's voice.

They turned to see a man dressed in brown-green cloth. He had a hood covering his head, carried a quiver on his back full of arrows, and held a huge bow. The children didn't waste any time, and ran in his direction. They all ran to a different part of the forest. Eventually the man said:

"I think we have lost him now!"

"Thank you" said Chloe. "That was really scary".

"No problem!" said the man smiling. He pulled his hood down to reveal his head; he looked tired and unshaven.

"Will you be alright now?" he asked the children. "You are close to a village here. I need to go before the Royal hunting party catch up with me; I don't think they like me poaching the royal boar and deer".

The children nodded. The man winked at them, put his hood back up, and then sprinted off between the trees and out of sight.

Daniel and Chloe had barely caught their breath when they heard the clip clopping of approaching hooves. Four men on horseback appeared.

"Daniel!" hissed Chloe "We need to go into invisible mode".

"No!" argued Daniel, "I want to carry on with this adventure!"

"Daniel!" insisted Chloe.

"What are you children doing here?" asked one man, sternly.

"Just going to the village" replied Daniel.

"I don't recognise you!" said another, "I think you have been poaching. The king has been losing a lot of his prize herd recently".

"We have no weapons or poached animals!" insisted Daniel.

"Let's arrest them, just to be sure" said the first man, smirking nastily.

Without wasting a moment, Daniel and Chloe started to run away, but they were still tired from outrunning the wolf. Chloe fumbled in her pocket to try to press the button on her compass to turn invisible, just as Daniel tripped over. Chloe found herself back in her garden in her own time, but Daniel was not with her. The compasses were supposed to be linked so that they would always travel together! Chloe quickly turned to invisible mode, and tried to go back straight away to find Daniel.

She arrived back in the forest to see the men shouting and cursing looking around them, but there was no sign of Daniel.

Chloe started to worry about her brother, she soon found the nice hooded man she had met earlier on. She made herself visible so she could speak to him.

The man was startled to be suddenly faced with a small girl with tears rolling down her face.

"Have you seen my brother?" Chloe asked.

"I did, don't worry I just helped him to escape from the king's men" said the man. "But then, he used a strange device to disappear".

"Oh thank you!" said Chloe, relieved. "He must have gone home!"

"How, what, oh never mind!" said the man confused. "Talking about home, I need to go over the mountains back the area of forest where I live, got plenty of food to keep me going" he smiled.

The man moved some ferns to reveal a small cart loaded up with the food he had poached from the forest. A few men appeared through the trees, and were leading some horses. One man was small, was dressed in brown, and had a bald patch on his head. There was a huge tall man with a beard, and there were a couple of other men dressed in green-brown clothes.

"Sorry Robin, the horses took an age to fill up with drink; we are ready to go now" said the tall man.

"Right you are John!" said the man known as Robin. "Can you find your way, young lady?"

Chloe smiled. "Yes, thank you. Have a safe trip home!"

She waved goodbye to the men, and used the compass to return back home. She went excitedly to find Daniel and to tell him about the other men she had met. There had been something strangely familiar about them, but she couldn't quite work out what it was.

Chloe ran into the house shouting for Daniel.

"He's not here" said her Mum puzzled. "I thought you two were out somewhere together?"

"Oh no" thought Chloe to herself, "Where on earth, and in time, is he?"

Chapter 2: The search for Daniel

Chloe sat in her room and looked down at the compass in her hands. How had she and Daniel become separated? She then looked at the extra buttons on her compass and remembered that the Professor had mentioned that there was a way of calling or re-linking to the other compasses. Maybe if she tried to call Daniel again, then she could find him.

Chloe pressed a button hopefully, and closed her eyes. She had not opened them, but could feel hot dry air gently blowing on her face, and could see the glow of the bright sun through her closed eye lids. She opened her eyes and gasped in amazement at the sight around her.

It was unmistakeable; the style of the people buzzing around her, the sand, and the huge pyramids - Chloe was in ancient Egypt.

Chloe walked along the street and glanced at all the young children to see if any might be Daniel in disguise. A few people turned to stare at the little fair girl who was wearing unusual and bright-coloured clothes.

As she continued to make her way down the crowded street, she heard a whisper.

"Pstt, Chloe!" said the voice, "Over here!"

Chloe turned around and saw that the voice had come from a man who was dressed in a stripy head dress, a huge golden belt and carried a huge staff in his hand. Chloe shrunk down in fright.

"It's me, Professor Bailey", the man said. "What are you doing here in Egypt, and where's Daniel?"

Before Chloe could answer, the Professor looked around him and noticed that some people were staring, puzzled about Chloe's appearance. The Professor quickly reached into a bag he was carrying and handed Chloe a wig and a loose top to put over her clothes, then they went to a quieter corner to talk.

"Daniel's lost!" sighed Chloe. "We were in Delamere forest back in the times when there were wolves and boar, we were chased by some men accusing us of poaching, then Daniel fell and I didn't see him again. A nice man we had met, I think his name was Robin, said that Daniel used his compass to disappear. I tried to call him, and ended up here".

"Hmm, worrying", frowned the Professor. "Your compass should have located Daniel's before it located mine. Daniel's compass is either broken or damaged. We have a chance if it isn't completely broken".

He got his own compass out of his pocket and played with some buttons on the back.

"We're in luck!" he smiled. "I think there may be a slight signal coming from Daniel's compass that we can track. We need to go somewhere high to not have interference from things around us. Now, where can we go?"

Chloe looked around and then spotted the largest of the pyramids, still being constructed, in the distance across the sand.

"Will that do?" she asked pointing across at the pyramid.

"Perfect!" said the Professor. "Let's be quick, no time to lose!"

He went up to a man who was holding the reins of two camels and said something to him in a strange language that Chloe had never heard before. Before she knew it, she was being shoved up onto the back of one of the camels.

"It's a bit far to walk in this heat!" said the Professor. "I've been learning Egyptian, and have just convinced the camel owner that we need these camels on urgent Pharaoh business; I am disguised as one of the Pharaoh's guards, after all.

Chloe and the Professor rode the two eager camels across to the pyramid, and were there in no time. When they arrived, there were lots of slaves working away in the midday sun building the pyramid. They backed off when they saw the Professor in his disguise.

The Professor spoke to one of the slaves, and then grabbed Chloe's hand.

"Come on!" the actual Pharaoh is about to turn up, if we are going to do this, we need to be quick!" urged the Professor.

They scrambled and climbed up the side of the pyramid. The rocks were warm and hard to climb. Chloe felt scared, but was determined to get to the top. Once at the top, the view was amazing; they could see for miles around. The heat caused the air to shimmer, almost like waves across the sand.

The Professor got out his compass and instructed Chloe to get hers out too.

"OK!" he said "We need to link our compasses together first, then see if we can get a good lock on Daniel's compass! Here goes nothing!"

The Professor twisted a few buttons and grabbed Chloe's hand.

A second later they were transported from the bright sun of Egypt. Chloe blinked her eyes as they adjusted to the darkness. It was still very warm, but in a horrible, damp, way.

"Where are we?" gasped Chloe.

They were in a small dank room, which had a very unpleasant smell. Chloe turned to see a figure sprawled out on a hard stone bed in the corner of the room. She tiptoed over. It wasn't Daniel, it was a middle-aged man dressed in a knight outfit. He didn't look very well; his cheeks were sunken in and he seemed to be in a delirious sleep.

"Need to...go home!" gasped the man, still with his eyes closed.

"Professor! Look at this man!" urged Chloe.

The Professor came over to look more closely at the man. He studied the symbols on the man's clothing and shield.

"Why, I believe this is a man called Sir Ro!" he said.

"He looks very ill", said Chloe.

"Yes, the story goes that he was near death after being captured in the Crusades far from home, he then wished to go home and mysteriously appeared right outside his castle in Cheshire.

"He's from Cheshire?!" said Chloe excitedly.

"Yes!" said the Professor, "Aha, well that could mean...."

"What does it mean?!" said Chloe.

"It means that I think Daniel is actually back in Cheshire and not here. The signal wasn't strong enough to get us back exactly to the right place, but it has brought us to someone who is a link to where Daniel must be. I am sure we are now in the right time, but we need to get back to Cheshire!"

"What about Sir Ro?" asked Chloe. "We can't leave him here!"

"We shouldn't really interfere with these things", replied the Professor.

"Yes, but can you explain the famous legend about how Sir Ro got back to Cheshire so mysteriously?" asked Chloe.

"I can't, unless he had a compass like… of course, well done Chloe! We must be destined to take him with us! We are actually part of the legend!"

The Professor gently took the hand of Sir Ro, and then slid the slider on the compass.

The three travellers were transported from the stuffy dark room to cool and leafy Cheshire. Chloe and the Professor helped Sir Ro to walk a few steps. Sir Ro still didn't seem totally conscious and was confused. They left him outside a little stone cottage, knocked at the door, and then hid at a safe distance. A lady came out of the cottage and found Sir Ro; she quickly put a blanket around him and got him a cup of water to drink.

Chloe and the Professor, watched from the trees; they wanted to make sure this point in history went as it was supposed to. Sir Ro would recover and go back to his castle, where he would shock a con artist who was trying to steal his wife and his castle, Sir Ro would get rid of him and be reunited with his beloved wife.

Chloe was glad that Sir Ro was going to be OK now he was home, but she still worried about Daniel. The Professor said that Sir Ro was the link, hopefully that meant that Daniel was somewhere nearby.

Chloe and Professor walked to a nearby village where there seemed to be some sort of event taking place. A few people stared at them as they walked through to the village square.

"Professor, we are still in our Egyptian outfits!" realised Chloe.

"Whoops, I didn't think about getting changed, we must look very odd!" said the Professor.

There were signs attached to some posts that read "Run the gauntlet and test your skills as a knight". There were a number of knights around setting up some equipment.

"Surely it's not a real running of the gauntlet" questioned Chloe, "Wasn't it used a punishment?"

"Maybe it's just a pretend one, look there are some children lined up ready" replied the Professor.

In the middle of the village there stood a huge wooden frame containing a series of big buckets, ropes, pulleys and spikes. A young boy stepped forward; he was wearing armour and carried a sword in his hand. A horn sounded, the boy ran forwards and was immediately knocked sideways by a huge bucket that swung down from the frame. He was not badly injured and stood straight back up again.

The next boy in the line stepped up. The horn sounded again; he missed the bucket, dipped under some hammers that swung around, jumped over some daggers sticking out, balanced across a rotating barrel and made it to the other side! The crowd cheered.

"Well done!" shouted one of the knights. "You will make a true knight one day!"

The boy took off his helmet and both Chloe and the Professor gasped; it was Daniel!

Chapter 3: The young knight

Daniel turned to see a two very odd looking people looking at him. Then he recognised the little one; it was his sister Chloe dressed in some sort of Egyptian outfit and funny black wig. He ran over to them.

"Chloe and….Professor, what are you doing here?" he gasped in surprise.

Chloe looked at Daniel; he looked different, maybe even a bit taller than she had remembered. She gave him a big hug.

"Daniel, we thought we'd lost you forever, what happened?" asked Chloe.

Before Daniel could reply, two knights came strolling over looking confused.

"Daniel, who are these people? Do you know them?"

Daniel thought very quickly.

"Yes, finally my sister and my long lost, erm, uncle, have returned from their travels". He said.

The knights looked at each other, frowned and then grinned.

"Ah, we thought they were dressed a bit strangely. You are both very welcome, it is nice to meet the family of our prodigy", they said.

"Prodigy?" whispered Chloe. "What HAVE you been up to Daniel?"

Daniel introduced the knights as Sir Gawain and Sir Venables. Sir Gawain had been stationed in Cheshire for a few months, and had found Daniel and taken him in. It seemed that for Daniel it had been a few months since the incident in the forest, but it was still the same very busy day for Chloe.

The knights explained that Daniel was of age and had been undergoing training to become a knight. Daniel gladly showed off his horse riding and weaponry skills. Chloe watched with her hands over her eyes because she was so nervous about the stunts Daniel was doing.

"Daniel's learned a lot in a few months" remarked Sir Gawain. "It often takes years for a knight to reach that standard. Why he'll be joining me in Camelot at this rate!"

"Camelot!" gasped Chloe. "You are Sir Gawain of the knights of Camelot?"

"Aha, my reputation must precede me" replied Sir Gawain. "Your brother will be good enough one day to be a knight of the round table.

Chloe turned pale as she thought about her brother becoming a knight.

"NO!" yelled Chloe. She made everybody jump in shock. "This has gone far enough, Daniel you need to come home right away!"

"Chloe!" moaned Daniel. "You heard Sir Gawain; knight, Camelot, round table!"

"A word in private, please Daniel!" said Chloe, dragging her brother off.

Sir Gawain laughed with the Professor.

"She's a feisty one, your niece; I think she should sign up to be a knight too!"

Sir Venables mumbled something about needing to do some dragon slaying practice and left the Professor and Sir Gawain to talk.

Chloe and Daniel found somewhere to chat; it was inside a grand looking tent that conveniently contained lots of delicious food.

"Chloe, my compass got damaged so I couldn't come home. I did want to, but now I'm training to be a knight" started Daniel. He then grabbed a roast chicken leg from the table next to him and started munching away.

"Yes, I know", said Chloe, "but you have already aged a few months in a day, how can I explain it to Mum and Dad if you don't come home and then return as a grown up man!" She then grabbed an apple from the table and ate it.

Daniel ate and thought about his life as a knight, and then thought about the comforts of home, being with Chloe and the rest of his family again.

"OK, you're right" he sighed. "I am glad to have learned so many skills, but my place isn't in these times or being a knight".

They left the tent through one flap, just as the chef returned through another entrance. He looked angrily at the discarded half eaten food that had been left behind. These knights were certainly a greedy lot, he thought.

Daniel and Chloe walked back to where Sir Gawain and the Professor were deep in conversation.

Sir Gawain turned when he noticed the children approaching.

"Ah, just in time to hear my tale about the green giant!" he said.

Sir Gawain talked about a giant green knight who he had battled. How he had been challenged to strike a blow and had chopped the green knight's head clean off, but then the knight had just picked up his head, and walked off - alive. He said that he would return a blow to Sir Gawain after a year and a day.

"When will it be a year and a day?" asked Daniel.

"Tomorrow, as it happens!" replied Sir Gawain. "That is why I have been staying in the area. I need to travel to a nearby castle tomorrow and I will face the green knight somewhere near there."

"Which castle do you need to go to?" asked the Professor.

"Beeston castle" replied Sir Gawain.

Daniel and Chloe looked excitedly at each other; what luck! Beeston castle was the very same castle that they knew well in the modern times and had also visited there during a siege in the past. Daniel and Chloe decided at that moment to just wait another day before returning home.

After a fun night camping in a tent; Sir Gawain, the Professor, Daniel, and Chloe, travelled to Beeston. Sir Gawain had warned them about the possible dangers. They travelled on horseback, with Chloe grabbing onto her horses reins very tightly as it trotted along the winding roads that led to the castle. When they arrived, they were greeted by the Lord of the castle and his beautiful wife.

The Lord showed them where they would be staying and made sure they were well cared for. He then quickly announced that he was going out hunting and that his guests should relax.

Sir Gawain went for a look around and the Lord's wife insisted on joining him to give him a guided tour. Daniel, Chloe and Professor Bailey relaxed on some comfortable seats in a large living room. The ceiling rose up in the middle to a central point, the stone walls were lined with various hunting trophies, and there was a huge open fire warming up the room.

The Professor sat on a stool, fixing Daniel's broken compass and occasionally peered out of a small window that led to the courtyard. He kept muttering "Hmm, very interesting!" to himself. Daniel and Chloe giggled at the eccentric professor.

Sir Gawain returned alone a short time later. He rushed into the room looking flushed and carrying a green sash in his hand.

"What is the matter, Sir Gawain?" asked Daniel.

"It's the Lady of the castle, she keeps trying to kiss me and then gave me this sash" he said.

"Eww!" said Daniel. "That's a bit strange!"

The Professor looked concerned. "Whatever you do, don't let her try to kiss you again!" he said. "There's something strange going on. I've been looking out of the window and have spotted a very strange old lady, who doesn't walk like an old lady should, she was there pacing around the courtyard."

"What do you mean?" asked Daniel and Chloe.

"I mean" said the Professor. "I don't think everything, and everyone, is at it seems here".

Just then there was a loud bashing at the door and a huge knight dressed in green came striding into the room.

"Aha!" shouted the green knight. "Sir Gawain, we meet again!"

Sir Gawain stood up and sighed. "Now to face death".

The Professor went to usher the children out of the room just as the green knight went to bring his axe down onto Sir Gawain, but the children stopped and tried to run up to Sir Gawain. The Professor had to hold them back. Daniel was very difficult to contain because he was now very strong and wanted to defend Sir Gawain.

The axe came down and they were shocked and relieved that Sir Gawain still alive, and sat rubbing a small cut on the back of his neck that had been made by the axe.

"That is for accepting the sash" bellowed the green knight. "You passed the test of not giving in to my beautiful wife by not letting her kiss you again, so I will spare your life".

"Wait, your wife?" asked Sir Gawain. Just then the green knight shrunk down and turned into the Lord of the castle. The Lord's wife walked into the room and winked at the astonished guests.

The Lord explained how he had been put under a spell by the evil witch Morgana, the old lady the Professor had seen was actually her in disguise. The Lord had been cursed to change into the huge green knight against his will, but now the curse was broken. The Lord's wife said that Morgana had just fled from the castle, so she knew the curse must be broken.

Daniel and Chloe were amazed. They had seen a lot in their adventures so far, but this was the strangest thing yet. They were glad that Sir Gawain was OK. The lord and the lady of the castle were very happy that Sir Gawain had rid them from the witch Morgana.

It was soon time to say goodbye, the Professor had fixed Daniel's compass, so it was time to go home. Sir Gawain was keen to get back to Camelot to tell the other knights about his adventures.

Daniel and Sir Gawain shook hands and said goodbye to each other; each had made a good friend in the other. Sir Gawain rode off across the drawbridge of the castle, the Professor unlinked his compass from Daniel and Chloe's, and then disappeared. Finally Daniel and Chloe returned home.

When they arrived at their house, their parents were shocked to see Daniel still in his knight outfit and Chloe dressed like an Egyptian peasant.

"What have you pair been up to, looks like a good party, whatever it was!" laughed their Dad.

"Daniel, I swear you have grown a few inches taller in a few hours" gasped their Mum, ruffling Daniel's dirty hair. "Hmm, you both definitely need a bath!"

Chapter 4: Higgins the highwayman returns

Daniel and Chloe had been having so many adventures around the world, they suddenly realised that they had forgotten to visit their old friend Charles the cavalier ghost in nearby Chester.

They decided to go to Chester in the time period they had visited before, because that was when they had seen Charles the most (and it was nice to see the bustling old streets of the city). The last time they had gone back they had had a run in with a highwayman called Higgins who was angry that they had once stopped him robbing a stagecoach and had then caught him trying to steal some jewellery from an open window in Chester.

Daniel and Chloe made their way through the streets and observed all the ghosts that lived there. The ghosts came from all different time periods going back to the Romans and the Celts before them. Their old friend Charles spotted the children as they came near and floated down from his favourite inn to see them.

"Great to see you!" he smiled. "I was so worried when I last saw you and you were being chased by that rotten highwayman! Glad you escaped from him!"

"Thanks for your help trying to stop him; it's a shame he couldn't see ghosts, and be scared away by you and your friends" said Daniel. "How long ago was that? It's hard to keep track with all this time travelling!"

Charles thought hard. "Hmm!" he frowned. "Must be about a year and a half ago I guess".

"I hope the highwayman is far away from Chester", said Chloe.

"He should be" said Charles. "Higgins has been in more trouble since you last saw him. He is now wanted for the murder of a rich Spanish woman and her maid. Apparently, he stole thousands of pounds worth of the lady's Spanish coins".

"It's a shame he wasn't caught by the police when we last met him" frowned Daniel.

"Anyway, enough of that!" said Charles, changing the subject, "I wanted to give you the full ghost tour of Chester; you haven't met all my friends yet! I've even made my peace with those pesky Parliamentarians I was fighting in the Civil war!"

Daniel and Chloe made sure they were in invisible mode because that meant they could travel straight through solid objects (like a spirit or ghost). They then had the most amazing tour exploring all the old crypts in the city, meeting lots of friendly ghosts, and Charles even worked out how to levitate them so they could see the city from the sky.

"This is so amazing!" they grinned. Charles took them flying over the rooftops and chimneys. After a couple of hours of an amazing tour, the children decided that they should go. The only problem was that Charles could not leave the boundaries of the city walls, so he could not leave to go with them. They thanked him for the adventure and said they would be back soon; while they still had some energy, Daniel and Chloe just wanted to quickly travel to the nearby coast of Wales before returning home.

They used their compasses to take themselves straight to where they wanted to go, and found themselves on an old road just close to the beach.

"Come on Chloe!" smiled Daniel. "Let's turn to visible so we can run barefoot on the sand and feel it between our toes!"

"OK" smiled Chloe undoing her shoes.

They ran across the sand, leaving behind their footprints and jumping over shells left behind on the sand. They both were so happy that they didn't notice a murky figure creeping up behind them until it was too late.

"So, we meet again!" said a snarling voice.

Daniel and Chloe spun around to find themselves face to face with Higgins the highwayman! He quickly grabbed Chloe, and held a pistol to her.

"I've never forgiven you pesky children, and I've got no problems with keeping you quiet, permanently! I'll also be having that device you use to make yourselves appear and disappear".

The thought of someone as evil as Higgins the highwayman having a magic compass made Daniel and Chloe feel even more scared.

Higgins loaded his gun and went to grab Chloe's compass. Then something amazing happened. Daniel suddenly leapt forwards and kicked the gun straight out of Higgins's hand. Daniel then gently pushed Chloe to the side and then managed to disarm a knife that Higgins had pulled out. For a boy so much smaller than the highwayman, his speed and strength was amazing. Daniel got Higgins into a headlock from which he couldn't escape. He then shouted to a shocked Chloe who was still tightly clutching her precious compass.

"Chloe, grab the pistol and fire it into the air, we need to get someone's attention!" shouted Daniel.

Chloe silently nodded and did as she was told. She lifted the gun and pointed it into the air and pulled the trigger. The bangs echoed around. Within a couple of minutes they heard shouting in the distance, as someone approached.

"I don't know how you did all that!" shouted Higgins, lying on the floor. "You're just a boy!"

Daniel smiled. "Yeah, but what you didn't realise is that since we last met, I've been having knight training with one of the best knights ever to walk the earth!"

"So, those devices allow you to time travel too?!" he snarled, eyes gleaming.

"Actually yes, but you'll never get chance to get your hands on one, that would be far too dangerous!" said Daniel.

The highwayman struggled, reaching out for the compass. Luckily, just then the people who had been approaching reached them; they were policemen. They had heard a gun shot, but then were bemused at the sight of a young boy holding down a fully grown man. They then realised who the man was; he was a very dangerous and wanted criminal.

"Higgins!" shouted one policeman. "We finally have you!"

"You've got nothing on me!" shouted Higgins.

"We have a warrant for your arrest, all we need is evidence that you committed murder", replied the policemen.

Daniel grabbed a money pouch from Higgins's belt and threw it to one of the men.

"Take a look in there, I think this will be all the evidence you need!" he said.

Sure enough, the bag was full of the stolen Spanish coins that could link Higgins to the murder.

The policemen led Higgins away. Daniel and Chloe were very relieved that he had finally been caught. Higgins didn't turn around as he went out of sight.

Daniel and Chloe sighed with relief, grabbed their shoes, and carried on with their planned walk along the beach.

"Daniel, you were amazing!" said Chloe. "What other skills did you learn?"

"Ooh lots!" said Daniel. "I hope in a way that I don't have to use too many of them!"

They turned to see one of the policemen coming back towards them.

"Hello again children" he said. "Thanks again for catching such a dangerous criminal. I forgot to give you your reward".

He handed them a big sack, and then waved and went away again. Inside the sack were lots of lots of coins (luckily not the stolen Spanish ones!).

"Cool, treasure!" smiled Chloe.

Daniel and Chloe went home again and hid the sack of coins in their room. Hopefully they would come in handy for spending money for their time travelling adventures!

Chapter 5: Aztecs

It was a rainy and cold Sunday afternoon. Daniel and Chloe were bored because they were stuck inside the house.

"Do you know somewhere I'd really like to see?" said Daniel.

"No, where?" yawned Chloe, she was feeling very bored today.

"Mexico!" said Daniel. "It would be lovely and sunny compared to the weather here today. Shall we go for a quick visit?"

Daniel turned to see Chloe already getting her shorts on and putting some sun cream on her face.

"Let's go!" she said.

They grabbed some of the old coins they had earned, just in case, and then used the compasses to take themselves to Mexico. They were in the middle of the capital, Mexico City. It was very busy and very hot.

"Time to go back a few hundred years to when it was quieter!" said Daniel turning the button on his compass.

They then found themselves in a much smaller city, with rivers instead of roads. There was an unusual looking temple in the distance.

"I think we are in the time of the Aztecs; cool!" smiled Daniel.

The two children walked down a busy market street. People were selling vegetables, ornaments and tortillas. Daniel went to try to buy a tortilla and showed one his coins to the seller. The man shook his head and pointed to a pot of cocoa beans.

"Oh no, I think they used cocoa beans instead of money!" said Chloe.

Just then a very important looking man appeared around the corner. He was in a funny box thing and was being carried inside it by four men. The man stopped when he saw the unusual visitors.

He gestured to the tortilla seller to give some of his ware to the children. Daniel and Chloe thanked him and bowed slightly. He tried to talk to them, but they couldn't communicate well. Another seller brought a drink over to them, Daniel took a sip. It was full of chilli and he spat it out when it burned his mouth. The man in the box laughed. He then gestured that he was moving on, so Daniel and Chloe turned to walk away.

Just then there were huge gasps and the people around them began to shout.

"What's wrong, do you think?" asked Chloe.

Daniel went red. "Uh oh, I think he is what is known as "The Speaker", I just remembered that you are never to turn you back to him…..quick, run!!"

A group of warriors carrying spears came running up. Daniel and Chloe ran up the steps of the temple. There were some Aztec priests there with huge blade and a few men that looked like prisoners.

"Oh no!" gasped Daniel. "I'm starting to realize this wasn't a good idea. Another thing the Aztecs were famous for was for their human sacrifices!"

"Now you tell me!" scolded Chloe.

Daniel grabbed a blade off one of the priests and struck and chopped through the chains of the prisoners, releasing them. He then pressed in the button on his compass to turn both Chloe and himself invisible.

The priests gasped at the magical disappearing children and then started to chant. The prisoners stood around, confused.

Chloe and Daniel walked around the city, still invisible. It was much more relaxing that way! As they wandered around they didn't notice one Aztec man turn and look at them and smile; Professor Bailey tried not to watch over them quite as much as he had at first, but he still liked to go undercover, just to make sure. He was glad that they had made the wise decision to go into invisible mode after the initial excitement they had caused. He could see them because, just like the children, he could now see ghosts (and spirit travellers) once he had used the compass.

Daniel and Chloe then casually used their compasses to go back home again. As far as adventures went, that had been a short, but quite an exciting one. What they didn't realise is that they were about to embark on their most unusual and exciting adventure yet.

Chapter 6: Dragon of Moston

Daniel was reading through one of his Mum's old folklore books. There was a tale of a dragon, who had caused mayhem nearby. Daniel told Chloe the tale and mentioned how it had been in a similar time to the one when they had seen Sir Gawain and the other knights.

"Daniel, I know what you are thinking!" said Chloe. "It sounds even more dangerous than visiting the Aztecs!"

"I doubt the dragon was even real" said Daniel, "We should go back and investigate the real event that started this strange folklore tale. I mean a dragon gobbling up people and being beaten by a knight, come off it! I know knights are very strong, because of my own experience, but it can't be true!"

They went back in time to a road now called Dragon Lane. Nearby was a lake that had been named Dragon Lake after the famous tale.

Daniel and Chloe were on a road that ran between two villages, and there wasn't much to see except fields and trees. Birds twittered in the trees.

"Hmm, it's very quiet" muttered Daniel. "Let's go and have a closer look at the lake".

As they wandered through the field, they heard a strange noise in the distance. Daniel quickly checked to make sure they were safely in invisible mode, just in case. The noise got closer; it was a loud swooping noise and there was a sound of shouting and a horse galloping.

Chloe looked up in the sky, a dark shadow passed by the sun just at that moment. She blinked and couldn't make out what the shadow was. Whatever it was then came around and passed by again.

"Chloe, I think the dragon story was actually true and wasn't just a made up fairy tale after all!" gulped Daniel.

Chloe saw the shadow getting lower; it was a creature with a long neck, wings, a long scaly tale and a big head with fire puffing out of its huge jaws; it was a real-life dragon!

"I think it wants to land here!" gasped Chloe.

Just then the shouting and horse noises got closer. Suddenly the field next to the lake filled up with people holding pitchforks and other tools. A man rode in on a horse; he was clad head to foot in armour and was wielding a huge sword.

The dragon landed clumsily and turned to face the man on the horse. It arched its back and puffed out fire towards the man. It then began to charge towards the man.

Daniel suddenly recognised the man; it was one of his knight friends, Sir Venables. Without a thought for safety, Daniel pressed the button on his compass to appear, grabbed a big pole from a shocked villager and ran towards the dragon.

"Daniel, come back!" yelled Chloe, above the noise of the crowd and the roaring dragon.

Sir Venables somehow got onto the back of the dragon and was wrestling it. He spotted Daniel and yelled.

"Daniel! Good to see you! I needed some help!" shouted Sir Venables.

Daniel hit the dragon's feet with his stick and leapt as the dragon swung its tail around to try to knock him over.

"This dragon's been eating people!" yelled Sir Venables. "We need to try to capture it!"

The knight grabbed some chains from his belt and threw one side down to Daniel. Daniel ran around the dragon trying to wrap the chains around it. The dragon was not happy as its legs began to get tangled up. It stretched itself and snapped the chains.

It then flew up into the air above the lake with Sir Venables still on its back. He struck it with his sword and the dragon plummeting into the lake with a huge splash.

Everyone stared in awe as the ripples came to a stop and noting emerged from the water.

"I think he killed it!" said one villager.

"He was a good, brave man" sighed another.

Just then there was a splashing sound, and Sir Venables surfaced from the water. He was pulling away the heavy armour around him and swimming with all his might to the edge of the lake. A cheer went up from the crowd.

"The beast is no more!" he shouted. Another cheer rose up from the crowd.

Sir Venables came to shore and people were congratulating him. Water poured out of gaps in his armour.

Chloe looked sad and was staring across at the still water of the lake.

"What's the matter?" asked Daniel, looking at Chloe.

"The poor dragon!" sighed Chloe.

"Chloe, it was eating people!" said Daniel.

"Well maybe it had a good reason, like it was protecting a nest or something!"

"Don't be silly Chloe" replied Daniel. "It was just a mean old dragon".

Daniel went to Sir Venables and they hugged and shook hands. Chloe sat still looking out at the lake. She turned to look at the bushes beside her and gasped as something caught her eye.

"I knew it!" she thought to herself. "The dragon came here because SHE was protecting this!" Hidden in the undergrowth was a huge egg.

"Everything OK now Chloe?" asked Daniel. He was enjoying the attention he was getting being known as the boy who helped a knight to slay a dragon.

"Yes fine" said Chloe. Blocking the view of the egg. "I think we should go home soon".

"OK, I'll just say goodbye to Sir Venables. He's going to be rewarded with a family crest with a dragon on. He also has some more coins for me as a reward to add to our collection."

Sir Venables approached Daniel, and suddenly looked serious again.

"Daniel, there is something I need to tell you about Sir Gawain", said Sir Venables.

"It's OK, we know he defeated the green knight" replied Daniel, not really listening.

Then disaster happened when Chloe went to her friend's house for tea and she had to leave the dragon behind. Daniel walked past Chloe's room and smelled a burning smell through the closed door. He ran in and the dragon had jumped out of the bed Chloe had made in her doll's pram and was hiccupping little fireballs all around the room. Daniel ran and got a bucket of water. Parts of the curtains and carpet were singed.

"Great!" sighed Daniel, looking sternly at the dragon. "Now, I'm going to have to take the blame with Mum and Dad for this because of you".

Daniel wrapped the dragon in a towel and hid the dragon in the chicken shed outside. He then had to lie to his parents and told them that he had been messing around with a candle, and took the scolding that followed.

Chloe came back from her friend's house, and when she saw her room, she realised straight away what must have happened.

"Daniel!" she whispered. "I know it was Bubbles, but where is he now?"

"Bubbles?!" sighed Daniel. "So that's his name. More like fire bubbles. He's in the chicken shed".

"The wooden, could easily go on fire chicken shed, with our pets chickens inside?" asked Chloe.

They ran outside. The shed looked to be in one piece. The door was open on the shed, so the chickens were running around their run. The chickens were not impressed with their new house mate, however, and were chasing it around. Bubbles flapped his wings and started to take off a little bit into the air. Chloe grabbed him quickly and hugged him.

"Right that's it!" demanded Daniel, getting his compass out. "We need to ask the Professor what we can do with this thing; it can't live here with us!"

Chloe felt sad and looked at her precious Bubbles the dragon, but she knew Daniel was right.

The call button on the compass hadn't been used before, and Daniel hoped that it would work. Literally within a couple of minutes, the Professor appeared in front of their eyes.

This time he has wearing some sort of beard wig, a strange pointy hat and animal skin clothes.

"Where have you been this time, Professor?" asked Daniel.

"Ah, just been blending in with Vikings. They are friendlier than people give them credit for" said the Professor.

The Professor looked in shock at the bundle in Chloe's arms.

"What have we got here?" he asked. "A young dragon, impressive! I'm surprised its mother let you take it away".

"It didn't...exactly" said Daniel, feeling a bit guilty. "Sir Venables and I fought the Mother dragon because it was eating people. She fell into a lake and didn't come out again.

"Ah, I see", frowned the Professor. "Well, they do act aggressively around their young. So this is the baby of the dragon of Moston then. I don't know how to look after dragons, I'm afraid, but I do know someone who does".

"Excellent!" shouted Daniel, "Let's go!"

"Hang on..." said Chloe, holding Bubbles even tighter. "This person isn't going to hurt him, I hope?"

"No, of course not, he's a dragon charmer", said the Professor.

The Professor linked the compasses and prepared to take them to another place.

"I don't think we need to go back in time; this person exists in lots of different times" said the Professor.

"Like Charles the cavalier ghost?" asked Daniel.

"Not exactly…" said the Professor, as he pressed the button on his compass.

They appeared on a sandy path, with ancient twisted trees around them.

"Wait!" said Chloe looking around her. "We are still in Cheshire, isn't this Alderley Edge?"

"Indeed it is" replied the Professor.

They walked along the path; there was a steep drop to one side. They soon arrived at a wall of rock. The Professor did a strange kind of knock; the rock sounded strangely hollow.

They heard a rustling in the trees behind them and turned to see an old man walking towards them. He had beady, but very intelligent looking eyes, and looked intently at the group. His eyes rested on the baby dragon snuggled up in Chloe's arms. He then turned to look at the Professor, who was stood, looking very odd, dressed in a Viking costume.

"Professor!" smiled the old man. "I nearly didn't recognise you with that strange beard on. Are you trying to out-do mine". He stroked his own long white beard, and chuckled.

"It's great to see you again, old friend! As you see, my friends have found a dragon" said the Professor.

"In this time, no more dragons exist. I'm guessing one of your special compasses was used to obtain this one" said the old man.

Then the old man paused, and looked at Daniel with a puzzled look on his face.

"Have we met before?" he asked Daniel.

"I don't think so?" replied Daniel.

"Yes, yes, I'm sure we have. Is your name not Daniel, did you run the gauntlet when Sir Gawain was in the area?"

"Yes, I am and I did. I got stuck in that time and Sir Gawain looked after me and trained me to be a knight" replied Daniel.

"And a fine knight you will become!" smiled the old man. "My name is Merlin by the way".

Chloe nearly dropped Bubbles when she heard the old man's name.

Merlin then turned to face Chloe.

"You have done a great job looking after this young dragon. I have a very important job for him to do. I need him to help me to guard something very important." said Merlin.

Chloe carefully handed the dragon to the wizard and then looked in shock as the wizard tapped the rock face in front of them.

"Daniel, I think you will be particularly interested in this!" said Merlin with a wink of his eye. The rock face rumbled, and then magically cracked open in front of them to reveal a dark cave.

Merlin got a candle out of his pocket and held it to Bubbles. Merlin then made some strange squeaking and clicking sounds. Bubbles seemed to understand and coughed on the candle. It lit immediately.

"Come on in!" said Merlin, waving his arm.

They walked through the cave. The floor was scattered with jewels and coins. As they got further in they were shocked to see what looked like statues of men and horses at the sides of the cave. One statue looked just like Sir Gawain; Daniel stopped and gasped.

"Ah, you've found him!" said Merlin, pausing. "As you've probably guessed, these aren't statues. These are actually Arthur and his knights frozen by magic. One day they will be released when Britain is at its greatest need. Don't worry, Sir Gawain is fine!"

Daniel paused and looked the frozen face of his good friend. He suddenly realised what Sir Venables had been trying to tell him by Dragon Lake.

Merlin then explained how he came regularly to the cave. It actually was part of a huge network of tunnels with a big cavern in the middle. Bubbles could live here and grow and Merlin would feed him and teach him to be a good dragon who could work alongside the knights when it was time for them to awake. He also said that Daniel and Chloe could visit whenever they wanted so that Bubbles didn't get lonely. With their compasses set on invisible mode, they could eventually take Bubbles out for a walk or fly.

They settled Bubbles down; Chloe gave Bubbles a big hug, and then left the cave. The entrance sealed behind them. Merlin told the children that he often walked around the edge, so should they need to enter the cave at any time, they should just look out for him.

Daniel and Chloe then returned home again, knowing that they would visit as often as they could to see Bubbles grow.

Back in the garden of the children's house, the Professor said his goodbyes and said they should call him at any time. He was nearly finished with his Viking studies and was hoping to go somewhere a bit warmer for his next trip.

Unbeknown to the group, Daniel and Chloe's Mum was also outside in the garden. She saw a man in a strange outfit talking to Daniel and Chloe, but then when she blinked, he had gone.

"Who was that, children?" asked Mum. Daniel and Chloe jumped in shock when they realised their Mum was there.

"Erm, just a man who accidentally came through our gate; I think he was looking for a Viking convention." said Daniel.

"Odd..." frowned Mum. "He looked strangely familiar. What was scaring the chickens?"

"I think they were just chasing a squirrel, Mum" said Chloe.

Their mother looked at them suspiciously. Mums always knew when their children were up to something. She couldn't quite work out what it was, but was soon going to find out.

Chapter 8: Famous inventor

The next day, Daniel and Chloe's Mum was busy tidying, and was trying to get rid of the black scorch marks in Chloe's room that, unknown to her, had been caused by a dragon.

She reached under the bed and put some dirty clothes into the washing basket. Something fell out of the pocket of Chloe's trousers. It looked like a watch; no, it was a strange looking compass.

Mum picked it up out of the basket and started to tap it; the dial didn't seem to point the right way to north. Daniel was in his own room looking at his compass and thinking about going back to see Sir Gawain again in a time before he was frozen.

Chloe spotted her Mum just in time as she pressed a button and dial at the same time. Chloe reached out to grab the compass, but was thrown to another place and time along with her Mum. Daniel appeared just next to them.

"Chloe, what are you doing....oh, Mum!" he said.

Daniel and Chloe's Mum looked around and blinked. She then looked at the compass and then at Daniel and Chloe.

"What on earth?" she started.

"Mum, we can explain everything!" said Daniel.

Just then the Professor appeared next to them.

"I've had a strange alarm saying that you have an additional passenger...oh!" he said, looking at Daniel and Chloe's Mum.

Mum stared at the Professor, confused.

"Wait, you were with the children yesterday, but you had a beard then. You are Professor Bailey!" gasped Mum.

Now it was Daniel and Chloe's turn to be confused.

"You know the Professor?" they asked.

"Of course, he used to teach my class when I was at university. I always loved his lessons because he always had strange artefacts from the past."

The Professor bowed. "Ah well, I could obtain them quite easily" he said with a wink of his eye.

Daniel and Chloe's Mum looked around at their surroundings. "OK, so somehow we have arrived in Venice by the looks of it. We went on holiday here a couple of years ago, do you remember kids? We seem to have appeared in a split second. Am I dreaming all of this?"

"No Mum, this is real!" said Chloe grabbing her Mum's arm. The compasses take us to different places…and back in time.

"I think I need a drink!" said Mum; she noticed some people dressed in old Venetian clothes walking past, and realised she was not in her own time. They found a café and had some drinks; luckily Daniel had some of his gold coins with him.

The children explained all about the compasses, how they worked and about all the adventures they had had so far. Their Mum gulped her drink and occasionally gasped at the dangerous adventures they had been involved in. At least now she understood how Chloe's room had got burned. She also took a huge interest in local myths and legends, so was amazed that so many of them were actually true.

While they were sitting in the café in the street, a man ran past their table and accidentally dropped something as he ran. Daniel picked up the parchment of paper that had been dropped, and it looked like a diagram of some sort of machine.

"Excuse me!" shouted Daniel, grabbing the paper and running after the man.

"Daniel, come back!" shouted his Mum, Chloe and the Professor. The man did not hear Daniel and continued to run through the streets. Soon there was a line of people all running in the same direction.

Finally after going up and down lots of little bridges that passed over the canals in the city, they saw the man disappearing down a narrow alley.

Daniel was first, and followed the man through a door into a workshop. The man turned in surprise when he saw a young boy standing behind him.

"You dropped this!" gasped Daniel catching his breath.

"Grazie" said the man, as he took back the parchment.

Suddenly Mum, Chloe and the Professor also piled through the door. The man suddenly looked very nervous and started to roll up papers that were lying around.

Daniel spotted some very familiar looking paintings on stands around the room. There were small models of strange contraptions that looked a bit like aeroplanes, helicopters and tanks, among other things.

The man started shouted something in Italian and was waving his arms around. The Professor replied in Italian and tried to calm him down.

"What are they saying Mum?" asked Chloe.

"I haven't got a clue!" replied her Mum, "But looking at these pictures and inventions lying around, plus the fact that we are in

Venice, leads me to believe that we are in the workshop of none other than Leonardo da Vinci!

The man calmed down after a few minutes. The Professor looked flustered, but excited at the same time.

"This is indeed Leonardo!" he grinned talking to the children and their Mum.

"I just had to persuade him that we were not rival inventors trying to steal his ideas!"

Daniel and Chloe looked in awe at all the strange and wonderful items around them. Leonardo even demonstrated some of his inventions to them once he realised he could trust them. He also spoke fairly good English to them, so the professor did not need to translate.

While everybody was busy watching and listening to Leonardo, they didn't notice a person sneaking in through the door at the back of the room, and quietly take something from the shelf. As the person crept out, he stood on some wood shavings on the floor and it made a loud crunching sound.

Everybody turned around and the thief paused for a second, but then ran out of the door.

"Quick, follow him!" shouted the Professor.

Leonardo was first out of the door, followed by the others. Leonardo went one way with the Professor, while Daniel Chloe and Mum tried to head him off using the next pathway along.

They ran over the big bridge that crossed the Grand Canal. Daniel could see the thief ahead, but he seemed to be getting away.

"This way leads to the lagoon!" shouted Mum, "He's probably got a get away boat moored there!"

Daniel suddenly came to a dead halt, Chloe and Mum piled into him from behind.

"Daniel!" exclaimed Chloe.

"I've got a plan!" said Daniel. "Quick, we need to set our compasses to invisible mode and then make sure we reappear at the edge of the city next to the lagoon. Ready?"

The compasses were set and Mum made sure she had hold of Chloe. The next second they were right where they needed to be, close to the lagoon.

Although there were a few boats around, there was one with the engine running and a shifty looking man aboard. Chloe, Daniel and Mum snuck onboard, still in invisible mode, and waited.

A minute later the man appeared, still with the painting under his arm. He leapt onto the boat. The Professor and Leonardo appeared, but they were too late as the boat started to sail away. Just then the boat jerked and came to stop; they had forgotten to undo the mooring rope. Daniel pressed the button on the compass to reappear. The two men fell back in shock and landed splash into the blue green water next to the boat.

"The painting!" yelled the Professor and Leonardo.

It floated painting side down in the water. Mum reached down and pulled it out. It was the infamous Mona Lisa painting! It looked unfinished, and the well-known lady in the picture was smiling more than she normally did.

"Oh no!" said Leonardo. "Now I will have to start all over again. The lady who models for me is not going to be happy!"

"Ah, I've got a feeling your next attempt is going to be even better than the first!" said the Professor smiling.

"It might look even better with her not smiling too much", added the Professor. He then turned at winked at the others because they all knew that the legendary Mona Lisa picture only showed a hint of a smile on the face.

The two thieves were hauled out of the water and were soon on their way to a Venetian jail cell.

"Great plan!" said everyone to Daniel.

Leonardo calmed down after a while and thanked everybody for their efforts. He rushed off to start the next version of what would turn out to be one of the most famous paintings in the world.

"What an adventure!" said Mum. "We should be getting back I guess!"

"Oh yes, we forgot to say, no time will have passed Mum!" said Daniel.

"Cool!" said Mum.

They said their goodbyes to the Professor once more. He had decided to stay in Venice for a little bit longer and spend some time with Leonardo.

Chloe set her compass for home. Daniel, Chloe and Mum then found themselves in Chloe's room.

"I think I may have just imagined all that!" gasped Mum.

Daniel suddenly realised he had something in his hand; it was one of Leonardo's small prototype helicopters in his hand. He held it up to show his Mum.

"OK, maybe not!" laughed Mum. "So, let me get this straight. We can go anywhere, in any time period and it will be as if no time has passed in the normal time".

"That's right" said Daniel and Chloe.

"Well, I think we should show your Dad! We could go to see family in Ireland, go for a day out to see you Aunty in Australia, or even...."

"Even what?" asked Daniel.

"What happens if you twist the button the other way, can you go to the future?"

"We haven't tried that yet!" yelled Daniel and Chloe excitedly.

Dad came up the stairs.

"What are you guys up to?" he asked.

"Hold onto this compass, and you'll find out. Ready guys?!" said Mum.

Dad looked confused.

"Don't worry Dad, we'll explain when we get there!" laughed Daniel and Chloe.

"Get where?" asked Dad. He saw the room in front of him disappear.

"Wow!" gasped Daniel and Chloe looking around them. "Welcome to the future!"

THE END